Mystery at
Winklesea

Other books by Helen Cresswell

Mystery at
Winklesea

HELEN
CRESSWELL

Illustrated by Susan Winter

*Hodder
Children's
Books*

a division of Hodder Headline

First published in Great Britain in 1995
by Hodder Children's Books

A Catalogue record for this book is available from the British Library

ISBN 0340 64643 8

Typeset by Phoenix Typesetting, Ilkley, West Yorkshire

Printed and bound in Great Britain by
Cox & Wyman, Reading, Berks

Hodder Children's Books
A Division of Hodder Headline plc
338 Euston Road
London NW1 3BH

Contents

For Fiona Kenshole with love

A Gift from Winklesea

One

Off to the Sea!

In everyday life, things might seem magic, but usually they aren't. You can slay a dragon on your computer, but when did you last see a fire breathing dragon in the supermarket? Pigs can't fly, it practically never rains mint sauce, and blue moons only come – well, once in a blue moon.

But the Kane family, who live at Number Seventeen Fetter Lane, know about *real* magic. It happened right out of the blue one night when they were eating their fish and chip supper. It didn't so much happen as hatch, out of a bluish green — or greenish blue — stone egg, that stood on a cockle-shell pedestal saying A GIFT FROM WINKLESEA in beautiful gold letters. So that is what they called the tiny creature that hatched out of it.

That had been last year. Since then, the Gift had swum away down the canal, and they thought they had lost him forever. But that summer they found him again, there in Winklesea, living with the sea-side donkeys.

Tomorrow the Kanes were off to Winklesea to collect the Gift. "Just think!" said Mary. "We'll have him for six whole months!"

The string of donkeys would winter inland in a field, but the Gift from Winklesea would come back to stay with the Kanes in their little house that backed onto the canal. That, after all, was where he had been born.

"It'll be like old times," said Mrs Kane happily.

Some mothers might not have been so pleased by the idea of such a visitor. The Gift had been small enough at the beginning, when he had first hatched out of the bluish green stone egg. A pocket dinosaur. They could all remember the moment as if it had been yesterday. They could still see that tiny grey head, and then the astonishing snap of the wide jaws when Dan offered a chip.

Since then the Gift had eaten literally thousands of chips – and crisps, and biscuits, and salmon sandwiches (his favourite) and cakes. At first he had seemed to double in size every day. By the time he had mysteriously disappeared from Fetter Lane he could only just squeeze into the wheelbarrow for rides. The Kanes had rather worried that he might end up the size of a house.

But when Dan and Mary had met the Gift again, at Winklesea, he looked exactly the same as when they had last seen him. He still ate at an astonishing rate – he could polish off a pork pie in a single gulp – but at least seemed to have stopped growing.

"Good job," Mr Kane had observed. "Or he'd have had to winter at Buckingham Palace."

"And eat the Queen's corgis!" Dan said.

"Never!" said Mary. "He never eats anything live."

This, too, was a good job. The Kanes'
neighbours would soon have organized
a petition if the Gift had started wolfing
down their pets. As it was, they needed
to keep a sharp eye on their dustbins.

By now, the neighbours knew that
there was to be a return visit by this exotic
creature. The Gift had appeared on television when he turned up at Winklesea,
and was quite famous. The people in
Fetter Lane were secretly rather proud
of this.

"Oh, we know him ever so well!" they
boasted to friends and relatives. They
had certainly sometimes passed him as
Dan and Mary trundled him along in
the wheelbarrow – and some of them
had chased him with pokers and yard
brushes when he came foraging in their
dustbins.

Uncle Fred was lending Mr Kane his
trailer for the Gift to ride home in.

"That'll do nicely, Fred," said Mr
Kane, eyeing it. "Just right, I reckon."

"Travel in style," said Uncle Fred. "But there'll be a few traffic jams when folks catch a sight of *him*!"

"They'll run into lampposts!" Mary giggled. "Think they're seeing things!"

"He'll like that," Dan said. "Proper show off."

Mary peered over the side into the dusty trailer.

"I'll put a rug in there," she decided. "And some cushions."

"Not mine, you won't," said Mrs Kane. "He'll be all over sand, and wet as like or not."

"Oh Mum! It'll rattle his bones!"

"W-e-ell . . ." Mrs Kane hesitated. She was as fond of the Gift as anyone, thought of him as her baby, almost. "Go on, then. I'll see if I can find an old blanket."

Off she went, while Mr Kane and Uncle Fred transferred the trailer from one car to the other.

"You're never bringing that silly thing here!"

It was Susie Barber, from next door. She had only moved in there a month ago, and already Dan and Mary wished she'd move out again.

"You're just jealous!" Mary told her.

Susie was an only child and her mother wouldn't let her have a pet, not even a hamster. She said they were smelly and brought germs into the house.

"Great big ugly thing!" said Susie. "Why don't you fetch an elephant home, while you're at it?"

"He's beautiful," Mary said. "Wait till you see him."

"Already have, thanks, on the telly," Susie said. "Looks like a dinosaur gone wrong. My mum says she might complain to the council."

"Why don't you go take a running jump, Susie Barber," Dan said. "Go boil your head."

She stuck her tongue out and went back into the house.

By now the trailer was in place and its number plate changed.

"The only thing is," said Mary, "what if it rains?"

"It'll not bother that one," said Uncle Fred. "In fact, all the better. Born to be wet. Miss the sea, I daresay."

"He's got the canal," Dan said. "Pity it hasn't got waves."

If Dan and Mary had known how to make waves on the canal they would have done it. They wanted everything to be perfect for the Gift's homecoming. For weeks they had been saving their pocket money to buy his favourite biscuits. They had cleared out the wheelbarrow and oiled its wheels. They had a surprise, too, had spent ages making it. At the moment it was still under Dan's bed.

Mr Kane had been busy too, preparing for their visitor. The Gift must have made his escape before by jumping over the wicket gate that led to the canal.

"Can't have that again," he said. "In any case, if he could jump it, so could anyone. Gift to burglars, that gate is."

And so he had spent hours out in the shed, banging and hammering, making a gate as high as the fence itself.

Later, they all sat round eating shepherd's pie. From time to time their eyes would wander to the framed photos of the Gift that stood on the mantelpiece, the television, the sideboard, alongside the school portraits of Dan and Mary.

"Eat up, Mary," said Mrs Kane.

"Excited, I expect," said Mr Kane.

"It's not that." Mary hesitated. "I mean, I *am* excited, but . . ."

"But what?" demanded Dan. "If you're not eating that, shove it over here. I will."

"Oh . . . Susie says her mum's going to complain to the council!"

"Oh yes?" said Mr Kane, spearing a carrot. "What about?"

"The Gift!"

"You what?" Mr Kane was choking on his carrot.

"Whatever for?" cried Mrs Kane.

"I don't know." Mary stared at her plate. "Being big, I suppose. And a nuisance. He did go knocking a lot of people's dustbins over. Oh – they won't take him away, will they?"

"Over my dead body they will," said Mrs Kane. "The very idea! If anyone wants reporting to the council, it's him!"

She meant Mr Barber, Susie's father. Nobody knew exactly what he did for a living. If asked, he would reply, "Oh, a bit of this, a bit of that."

"Only been here a month, and already his yard's like a scrap heap! I'll give him a bit of this, a bit of that!"

"No law against keeping pets," said Mr Kane. "And at least he don't yap, like that blessed peke at Number Nine."

All the Gift ever did was whimper softly when he was sad, and let out high, excited yelps if he was happy. There could not possibly be a law against that.

"So you eat up and forget all about it, Mary," said Mrs Kane. "Your father and I'll worry about that. We've brought you two up all right, and we can manage another, I daresay."

She really did think of the Gift as her baby.

"Early night tonight," she said, as she cleared the plates and brought out the treacle tart.

"Up at the crack," agreed Mr Kane.

"You sure you've got everything ready?"

Dan and Mary exchanged glances. Already their swim things, the kite and beachball were stowed in the boot of the car. But the surprise was still under Dan's bed, and that might take some time to arrange properly.

Straight after supper they went upstairs.

"You go into Mum and Dad's room and open the window," he instructed. "And get ready to catch the end when I push it over on the rake."

Mary nodded.

"Got the drawing pins?"

It turned out not to be as tricky as they had expected. Five minutes later the surprise was in place.

"Let's go and look!"

They raced downstairs.

"Mum, Dad, come and look!"

"Where?"

"In the street! Come on!"

"Trailer not vanished, I hope." Mr Kane put down his newspaper and followed them. Mrs Kane came too, still wiping her hands on the tea towel.

"Now — look!"

It was perfect, just as they had imagined. The banner hung right across the front of the house, and on it in bold red letters was the message:

WELCOME HOME WINKIE

Two

Seeing Double

Dan and Mary enjoyed the journey to Winklesea. There were bacon sandwiches to eat, and the usual singsong, with everyone joining in. When they had run out of favourites – *We're off to see the Wizard*, and *I Do Like to be beside the Seaside*, they launched into nursery rhymes. They sang *Wee Willie Winkie* and *Winkle Winkle Little Star*. Every now and then Mary peered over her shoulder to make sure the trailer was still there.

In no time at all they were craning for the first glimpse of the sea. Then, suddenly, there it was, blue and glittering, and they burst into a last triumphant chorus:

I do like to be beside the seaside,
I do like to be beside the sea!

"Straight to the prom, Alfred!" said Mrs Kane.

He drove carefully through the narrow, cobbled streets. They were still crowded with families trailing buckets and spades and licking ices. When word went round that the Gift was there every day on the sands, with the donkeys, the number of visitors had doubled overnight. On Bank Holidays, the police had to direct the traffic.

But tomorrow the children went back to school, and the town would be deserted and the sands bare.

In the car park Dan and Mary left Mr and Mrs Kane to unload and raced on ahead, making for the pier. That was where the donkey rides started.

When they got there, they stood panting and scanning about for their first glimpse of the Gift. There went the donkeys in the distance, led by Sam and Mr Tonks. A knot of people stood by the sign: DONKEY RIDES THIRTY PENCE.

"But where's Winkie? Where's *his* sign?"

There should be another sign that read: STAR ATTRACTION: TAKE A REAL LIVE MONSTER FOR A WALK – FIFTY PENCE. HAVE YOUR PHOTO TAKEN WITH HIM – TWENTY PENCE.

"There!" Dan pointed.

The sign was there, all right, but lying flat on the sand with Mr Tonks' jacket thrown over it.

"Oh no! No! He can't – he can't have . . ." Mary's view of the beach began to blur.

"Let's find out!"

They scuttered down the warm, sandy steps and ran to meet Mr Tonks, who was leading his donkeys back to the pier entrance.

"Mr Tonks!"

"Hello, there!" he said. "So here we are again! Bad pennies."

"Where is he?"

"Where's the Gift?"

"Just let me finish what I'm doing," he said, "and I'll tell you."

So Dan and Mary were forced to turn and go slowly back with the ambling donkeys. Mary remembered how much she loved them, with their huge furry, nodding heads and sweet hay smell. On their week's holiday Dan and Mary had been with them every day, and knew them all by name.

"Oh Rosie!" Mary patted the thick fur. "Oh Billy and Jacko – do you know where he's gone?"

The donkeys went patiently on, their huge fringed eyes giving no sign.

By the time they reached the pier Mr and Mrs Kane were dropping their bulging bags on the sand.

"Where is he?" cried Mrs Kane. "Where's my lamb?"

"Off duty, is he?" said Mr Kane.

Mr Tonks picked up the sign that said GONE TO LUNCH. BACK IN ONE HOUR, and propped it against the sea wall. He seemed amazingly calm and unhurried for someone who had lost his Star Attraction.

"Now then," he said. "Keeping well, are you?"

"Where *is* he?" Mary felt she might actually burst with impatience.

"As to that," replied Mr Tonks, "your guess is as good as mine."

They stared, all four of them, trying to take it in.

"But he'll be along when the fancy

takes him, whenever that might be. Oh yes – you won't catch him missing his grub!"

Part of the fun for the visitors was feeding the Gift. They tossed pork pies, buns, sandwiches and apples to see the Gift neatly field them, his wide mouth opening and shutting like clockwork.

"He hasn't disappeared?" Mary burst into tears.

Mrs Kane produced a handkerchief, and they all sat down on the sand. Between bites of his sandwiches Mr Tonks told them his story.

It had all begun a couple of weeks back, he said. One morning, when Mr Tonks and Sam had led the donkeys up the beach for the day's work, the Gift had not appeared as usual.

"Thought he'd overslept," he said. "Hasn't got a watch, of course, I know that. Thought he'd turn up in a bit."

But ten o'clock had come, eleven

o'clock, twelve, and still there was no sign of him.

"Began to think he'd gone, just like you did. But oh no – all of a sudden – there he was! Heard this great cheer go up, and clapping – and there he was! Queue for him a mile long by then, of course."

"But where had he been?" asked Mary.

"Now, you know better than that," he told her. "Bright as a button he may be, I grant you – but talk? No, not exactly."

The same thing had happened the next day, it seemed, and every day since. No sign of the Gift first thing, but then, sooner or later, there he was.

"Bit of a mystery, that," observed Mr Kane.

"Ah, but there's more of a mystery," said Mr Tonks. He took a bite of his sandwich and chewed thoughtfully. The others waited.

"Don't wear specs, as you can see," he said at last. "But beginning to think I ought to."

"Why's that then, Tonks?" asked Mr Kane.

"Double. Seeing double, if I'm to believe my eyes."

"Oooh, *that's* nasty!" cried Mrs Kane. "Get them tested, I should!"

"Only thing is," Mr Tonks continued. "Sam – he's seeing double as well. Ain't you?"

Sam, who had brought his own string of donkeys back, and fetched himself a beefburger, nodded, cheeks bulging.

"Could be infectious," said Mrs Kane doubtfully.

"Ah, but we don't see *everything* double," said Mr Tonks. "Oh no. Only him."

"Who?"

"The Gift," he said. "That's who."

"*I* seen two of him!" said Sam thickly. "Out there!"

He jabbed a finger in the direction of the sea, out by the pier's end.

"And I seen two over there!" Mr Tonks pointed far down the beach, towards the caravans in the dunes where the Kanes had stayed.

"But never close up, see. If I was to see two now, right here, next to them donkeys, that'd be a different thing. If it

was that close up, I'd *know* I was seeing
what I thought I was seeing."

"I can see that," agreed Mr Kane. "I
daresay I would, and all."

"Here soon," said Sam. "Usually here
by the time we've had us dinners."

"I'm going to watch, then!" said Mary.
"You look that way, Dan, and I'll look
this."

"We don't want you seeing double,"
said Mr Kane. 'Not at your age."

"Get me a deckchair will you, Alfred,"
said Mrs Kane. "I can't knit unless I'm sat
properly."

She took her knitting everywhere with
her. Mr Kane said that if you put everything she'd knitted end to end, you could
probably line the M1 with it.

"Oooh – I'd forgotten – got some
thing for you, Mr Tonks."

She delved in her bag and fetched out
a green woolly hat with matching scarf
and gloves. "For the winter, see."

"Oh very nice. Very nice indeed." He

tried on the hat. "Snug as a bug. That's very kind of you, Mrs Kane, and thank you."

"I'd have done something for the donkeys as well, but I couldn't think what."

"Ears stick up too much," agreed Mr Tonks. "No necks, to speak of, and no fingers."

"It's the same with the Gift," she said.

This was true. There was no knitting pattern on earth she could adapt to fit him, with his curved, spiny back and wing-like flippers.

"There!" screamed Mary. "There!"

They all looked over to where she was pointing. There, bobbing in the waves by the pier's end was a sleek grey head like that of a seal.

"Hurray!"

Dan and Mary scrambled to their feet and raced over the sand towards the sea's edge. By the time they reached it he was there, emerging from the waves, curling whiskers, bright boot button eyes and all.

"Winkie! Oh darling Winkie!"

He tilted back his head and let out a high, excited whoop of delight. His tail thrashed to and fro in a shower of spray.

Next minute Mary was hugging him and getting soaked and not caring a bit.

"Good boy, Winkie," said Dan gruffly. "Good old boy!"

The Gift nuzzled them both and playfully butted them with his head.

"You're coming home with us today!"

"And we've got a surprise for you!"

"And your favourite biscuits!"

They really did believe that he understood every word they said. He was, after all, magical — like no other creature on earth.

As the three of them hurried back up the beach a cheer went up on the sea wall. The Gift arched his neck and whinnied. He was a Star Attraction and this was his public.

Already apples and biscuits were flying through the air, but the Gift went straight to Mr and Mrs Kane. He very nearly knocked over their deckchairs.

"Oh my lamb! Bless his little heart!" Mrs Kane dabbed at her eyes.

"Well then, old chap," said Mr Kane. "Looking in the pink, and no mistake."

"It'll be the sea air," said Mrs Kane. "It'll have built him up."

"It's certainly given him an appetite," agreed Mr Kane.

The Gift was mopping up the fallen apples and biscuits, and now looked hopefully up to the line of admirers on the prom.

"Winkie!"

"Here!"

"Catch!"

The show had begun. The Gift darted this way and that, neatly fielding sausages, hard boiled eggs, tomatoes.

"You wonder where it all goes," remarked Mr Kane, not for the first time.

The show over for the time being, Mr Tonks took his jacket from the sign and propped it up again. The afternoon's business had begun.

It was just like old times. The Gift posed for his photograph with one family after another. Mary slipped on the rope halter so that it fitted neatly between two ridges of his spine, and he was ready to be taken for walks. Some of the children who led him were tiny, only four or five years old.

"Still don't think Tonks should call him a monster," remarked Mr Kane, "selling point or not. A proper monster'd be *eating* them kiddies, not toddling along side 'em meek as a lamb."

"He *is* a lamb," said Mrs Kane happily – and that was not for the first time, either.

As the shadows lengthened over the sands and the air chilled Mr and Mrs Kane folded their deckchairs, and Mr Tonks went for his last turn along the beach that summer. He gathered the donkeys together.

"Off on *their* holidays now," he observed.

Mary hugged them one after another, and whispered into their long, furry ears.

"See you next year!"

The Kanes and Mr Tonks shook hands.

"Look after him," said Mr Tonks. "Gold mine, that one."

"Live off the fat of the land," promised Mr Kane, and "of course we will, the pet!" cried his wife.

Mr Tonks went one way with the donkeys, and the Kanes the other, towards the car park. Mary led the Gift by his rope and a crowd of admirers followed them all the way.

"Here we are, then!" said Mr Kane, as they stopped by the trailer. "Fit for a king!"

"And there's a nice warm blanket in there," added Mrs Kane.

The Gift peered over the side of the trailer and saw the rug, and a rubber ring, one of his favourite toys. (Mr Kane had said that playing with rubber rings in trailers was against the Highway Code, but Mary had put it in anyway.)

They waited for him to scramble in. Instead, he turned away, and looked back at the sea, still glinting in the low sunlight.

"We all feel like that at the end of the holidays, old chap," said Mr Kane sympathetically.

"You're coming home with us," Mary told him. "Home!"

The Gift seemed hardly to hear her. Still he gazed out over the waves, and his eyes were so mournful that she could hardly bear it. As she watched, something glinted at the corner of his eyes and rolled down his face.

"Oh Mum – he's crying!"

"There, there!" Mrs Kane fetched out her handkerchief and dabbed gently at his eyes. "There, there, soon be better."

"Up we go – oops a daisy!" Mr Kane half lifted the Gift, and obediently he slithered over the edge of the trailer and flopped onto the rug.

A cheer went up from the spectators.

"Now you stop there, like a good boy!" Mrs Kane wagged a finger at him.

"No alighting while the vehicle's in motion," added Mr Kane.

"Oh Mum – can't I go in with him?" Mary begged.

"No you cannot," said Mr Kane. "Against the Highway Code."

So Dan and Mary climbed into the back of the car, and Mary held her breath for fear that the Gift would jump out, and disappear again. Mr Kane started the engine, the car began to move. Everyone in the car park waved or tooted their horns, and a chorus of voices followed them.

"Goodbye, goodbye Winkie!"

"Safe journey!"

"See you next year!"

As the car turned on to the road people were still running after them, cameras clicking. The Gift from Winklesea was a Star Attraction to the last.

Three

Police!

As Uncle Fred had predicted, the Gift caused quite a stir on the roads. Right from the start he seemed to like standing up, rather than lying on the rug. At first, they thought they could see why. He was watching the sea. Even as they left the cobbled streets of Winklesea behind, he craned his head this way and that, straining for a glimpse of it.

Long after the last sighting he kept

turning his head hopefully. Now and then he whimpered softly.

He seemed not to notice the attention he was attracting, or at any rate, not to mind it. If he had, he could easily have lain down on the rug, out of sight. Mary and Dan wanted to kneel on the back seat and watch in comfort, but Mr Kane would not let them.

"Against the Highway Code," he said. "Clunk click every trip!"

So they had to peer uncomfortably over their shoulders, and even then they had only half a view.

"Pity we haven't got necks as long as his," Dan said.

Every car that came up behind them pipped its horn. Through the windows of each car that passed they could see disbelieving faces and popping eyes. Some cars raced by, then stopped ahead of them. Then people leapt out with their cameras, hoping for a shot of this amazing sight.

Sooner or later someone was bound

to think that a Gift from Winklesea in a trailer was against the Highway Code.

A flashing blue light appeared behind them.

"Look out, here comes the fuzz!" yelled Dan.

At first the police car drew in behind and followed them. Through the windscreen Dan and Mary could see the faces of two policemen who had never, in all their years in the force, seen such a sight. The Gift obligingly turned their way. He was fascinated by the blue light, you could see that. He kept tilting his head this way and that, and making little jumping movements.

With a sudden swoop the police car was past them, and then drew in ahead, and stopped. A sign appeared in red lights: POLICE PLEASE STOP.

"Wow! We're nicked!" said Dan.

Mr Kane obediently put his foot on the brake.

"Oh Dad, they won't arrest us, will

they? They won't take him away?"

"Nothing about it in the Highway Code," he said. "Can't be."

Mary was sure that this was true. Whoever had drawn it up could never have imagined anything like this. Mr Kane was very keen on his Highway Code, and Mary had looked at it herself once or twice. It was all about things like "If you need to change your lane, first use your mirrors," and "Watch out for motor cyclists, cyclists and horse riders." So far as she could see there was nothing about Gifts from Winklesea.

Both officers got out of the car and came over. Their eyes were fixed nervously on the Gift, who had swivelled round to follow the flashing blue light. Mr Kane wound down the window.

"What seems to be the trouble, officer?" he asked – as if he didn't know.

"We weren't speeding," put in Mrs Kane. "Alfred never speeds."

The police were not even listening. Their eyes were still fixed disbelievingly on the Gift, now peering at them over the roof of the car. When they had first received a call that a prehistoric monster was travelling in a westerly direction between Anderton and Belford, they had thought it was a hoax.

"Or some old biddy needs her eyes testing," said One.

"Or some kid with Jurassic Park on the brain," said Two.

Now, they were not so sure. This creature regarding them with bright, inquisitive eyes, did have a certain prehistoric look about it.

"If it is a dinosaur, it's only a baby one," muttered One. "They're a lot bigger than that."

Two produced his notepad and pen.

"Seems harmless, at any rate," he said, though he was still poised to run, if need be. He dreamed of being a hero, that was partly why he had joined the police force, but had no ambitions to be a dead one.

Mr Kane took out his licence and insurance, though nobody had asked for them. He passed them through the window.

"I think you'll find they're in order," he said.

Police Officer One took them without a glance.

"Er – what is that you have in the trailer?" he asked.

"The Gift from Winklesea," said Dan and Mary in chorus.

"And he wouldn't hurt a fly," added Mary.

"He's a lamb," confirmed Mrs Kane.

"We're just taking him home for the winter," said Mr Kane, as if that explained everything.

"Er – has he got a licence?" asked Two.

"He's not a *dog*!" said Mary.

"I can see that," said Two. "So what exactly is he?"

"Ah," said Mr Kane, "that's a long story, that is."

Nevertheless, it had to be told. In the end, all the Kanes got out of the car and told bits of it in turn, right from the moment when Dan and Mary had spotted the greenish blue stone on its pedestal of cockleshells in the gift shop window.

All the while Two made notes, and all the while a traffic jam was building up, both in front and behind. The combination of flashing blue light and what looked like a baby dinosaur in a trailer, was irresistible. People were drawing up, leaving their cars and coming to investigate. Some had brought their cameras. Soon the Gift was posing obligingly. He tossed his rubber ring into the audience. A delighted child threw it back, and he arched his head and caught it. There was a burst of applause. The Gift was in his element.

"The Gift from Winklesea Road Show!" said Dan.

"Admission free!" added Mary.

"That's if you don't count the fines for causing an obstruction," said one of the officers.

"Right, everybody, that's it!" shouted the other. "Move along now. Show's over!"

Reluctantly the bystanders began to return to their cars.

"I reckon he's going to need an escort," said One. "Radio back to base and tell 'em we've got an emergency."

And so it was that an hour later the Gift from Winklesea arrived home in triumph, escorted by a police car, blue light flashing.

"Just like royalty!" said Mrs Kane happily.

As they turned into Fetter Lane people out washing their cars straightened their backs and stared. Net curtains twitched at the windows. By the time the cars drew up at Number Seventeen there was a small crowd to clap and cheer.

The police got out of their car and looked up at the red and white banner:

WELCOME HOME WINKIE

"Aren't dreaming, are we?" said One.

"All in a day's work," said Two. "Wish my kids could see him."

"Better not," said the other. "Only go wanting one for Christmas."

The Gift, too, was gazing up at the banner. It was hard to tell whether or not he was smiling.

"He can read it!" said Mary. "I'm sure he can!"

"Gets the message, anyhow," said Mr Kane. "Come on, old chap – down we come!"

The Gift obligingly slithered out of the trailer and there was another round of applause. Mrs Kane was already unlocking the front door.

"Cup of tea, officers?" she asked.

"Er – no, better not," said One. "But – there is just one thing . . ."

He looked rather sheepish.

"You don't happen to have a camera handy?"

"Course we do!" said Mr Kane, opening the boot of his car. "Never travel without one."

"It's just that Steve and me here, we thought . . ."

"I get it," said Mr Kane. "Want your picture taken with him."

"To show the lads at the station."

"And the kids."

"Say no more," said Mr Kane. "Hand him the rope, Mary."

The officers stood one each side of the Gift and posed happily, feeling like ten year olds again.

Click.

"Nice one," said Mr Kane. "Another for luck."

"Hang on a minute," said One. "Here!"

He took off his peaked cap and placed

it on the Gift's head. The bystanders laughed and cheered and wished they had their own cameras handy.

Click.

"Impersonating a police officer!" said Mr Kane. "Going to book him?"

The police said they would call in a few days for the photos.

"And I shouldn't go driving him about in that," they said. "Road hazard."

"Straight back to Fred in the morning," Mr Kane promised. "He's home now. No need for it."

The police drove off, and Mr Kane fished in his pocket.

"Here you are," he told Dan and Mary, handing them the money. "Straight down to the chip shop!"

It had already been decided that this would be their celebration supper. The Gift, after all, had hatched while the Kanes were eating fish and chips, and that had been his very first meal.

Dan and Mary set off at a run. Mr Kane's voice came after them, "and double chips for the Gift!"

Four

Homesick

That evening was like old times. The Gift from Winklesea followed Mr Kane into the house and knew at once that he was home. He went straight to the kitchen, and straight to the tin where the biscuits were kept. He nudged it back and forth, back and forth. This was an old trick.

"You don't want them now," Mrs Kane told him. The kettle was already

on and she was putting plates in the oven
to warm. "Spoil your supper."

This was unlikely. Eating was his
favourite thing in the world. It was his
hobby.

"Put the cloth on, Alfred, and lay the
table," said Mrs Kane. "They won't be
long."

The Gift followed Mr Kane into
the living room. He wasn't so much
following *him*, as the knives and forks.
Where there were knives and forks, there
was usually food. Once he realised the
table was bare he went over to the
mantelpiece and gazed at the bluish
green – or greenish blue – stone egg.
Mr Kane had glued it together again after
the Gift had hatched, and it still stood in
pride of place between the clock and the
green glass cat.

"He remembers!" said Mary.

She had left Dan in the queue and
raced back.

"Does he really, do you think?"

"Don't see why not. Elephants never forget, and he's not far off being one.'

"But he was only a baby! I can't remember being in my pram."

Now the Gift was moving about the room and peering at his photographs. There he was – in the fish tank, riding in the wheelbarrow, wearing his rosette from the Pet Show. And now Mary was certain he was smiling.

She ran and put her arms around him. "Oh Winkie! I do love you!"

"He don't want to know that," Mr Kane told her. "He wants his supper."

Soon it was there – cod and chips five times with an extra portion of chips for the Gift. His special bowl was empty before anyone else had half finished. He stood by the table, nose twitching, and bright eyes fastened on the half empty plates.

"Bottomless pit," observed Mr Kane. He tossed a chip and the Gift fielded it. That was half the fun of feeding him.

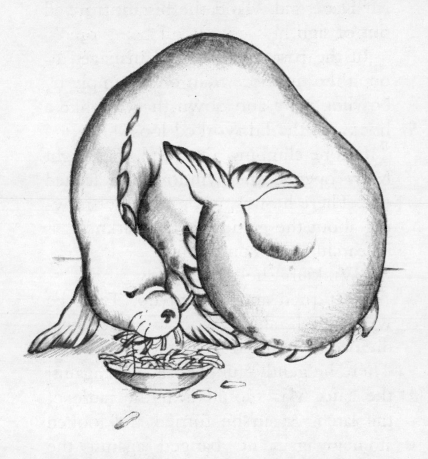

That night, and every night till the weather grew cold, the Gift was to sleep in the garden. Later, when the frosts came, he would come into the kitchen.

"Padlock on the bread bin, I daresay,"

Mr Kane said. "And the biscuit tin well out of sight."

In the past the Gift had managed to open the tin more than once, simply by bowling it up and down the yard like a hoop, till the lid worked loose.

Before climbing into bed that night Mary opened the window and leaned out. There he was, not asleep, but moving about the garden in the darkness, as if searching for something.

"Winkie!" she called softly.

He turned and looked up. Then he went to the high wooden fence that divided the garden from the canal bank. There he gently nudged his head against the gate. Mary could hear the rattle of the latch. Again he turned and looked at her, again he banged against the gate. It was clear what he was telling her.

"No!" she called. 'No, not now! To-morrow!"

To make her meaning clear she shut

the window. As she climbed into bed she thought she heard him whimper softly.

"Homesick, I expect," she thought. "For the sea. Bound to be, at first."

She remembered how longingly he had gazed back at it as he rode away from Winklesea in his trailer. If she had gone down and opened that gate, would he have jumped straight into the canal and followed it all the way back to the sea?

"Better not let him go in there," she thought. "Not for the first few days, anyway."

She fell asleep. When she woke it was not yet morning but still dark, and so at first she thought she was dreaming. She was dreaming that she was in a forest being pursued by baying wolves. But she was in her room, she could see the moon lighting the pattern on the curtains. The wolves were still there. It came again, that long, melancholy howl.

"The Gift!"

In a flash she was out of bed and at the window. There he was, brushed with silver, a creature of magic, strange beyond words in that little garden with its tall hollyhocks and glinting coldframes. His long neck arched as he threw back his head and howled at the moon.

"Winkie!"

He did not hear her, or if he did, he made no sign. Again that smooth grey head went back. Again came that howl that seemed to hold all the sadness and loneliness in the world. Mary could not bear it.

As she went onto the landing the light came on and she blinked, dazzled.

"Whatever . . . ?" She heard her mother's voice.

"It's Winkie!"

"What's up?" Now it was Dan's voice.

All four of them stumbled down the stairs. Mr Kane fumbled with the locks of the back door. Then they were out in the moonlit garden, barefoot and bemused.

A window was thrown open.

"What the devil? There's some trying to get some sleep round here!"

It was Mr Bit of This Bit of That from next door. His wife's face appeared behind him as the Gift howled again.

"Oooh that horrible noise – it goes right through you! Shut it up, can't you?"

Mary ran to the Gift and touched him gently. He turned his head but his eyes seemed not to see her at all. It was as if they were fixed on some far horizon.

"Come on,'" she said softly. "Come on. He can come inside, Mum, can't he?"

"Of course he can, the lamb! Whatever's the matter with him?"

"Not too many chips," said Mr Kane. "Had twice that, before now."

"There ought to be a law against it!" came Mrs Barber's voice.

Still the Gift stood there. He seemed to hear and see nothing. Dan came up behind Mary.

"Good boy, Winkie! Come on!" He shook the biscuit tin. That did it. All at once the Gift from Winklesea came back from wherever he had been. His silvery eyes fixed on the tin, his neck craned eagerly.

Rattling it, Dan turned and went back into the house. The Gift followed.

"Well!" said Mrs Kane, as they all stood round in the kitchen. "Never done that before!"

"He could be lonely," Mary said. "He couldn't sleep in my room, could he?"

"No," said Mrs Kane. "He could not. It's not hygienic."

"You sound just like Mrs Barber," Mary told her.

"If he makes that racket every night, she will report us to the council," Dan said.

Mrs Kane spread the rug from the trailer for the Gift to sleep on. Dan hid the biscuit tin in a cupboard and they all trooped back upstairs.

Mary went over to her open window and gazed out over the moonlit garden and silvered roofs beyond the canal. To the left she could see the broad shine of the canal itself, and – she stiffened. She stared. It was impossible, of course. The Gift was downstairs in the kitchen, tucked up for the night. She shut her eyes, then opened them again.

Still there! What else could it be,
rearing up out of that polished water?
Then she remembered what Mr Tonks
had said, and Sam.

"Seeing double!'

She blinked her eyes fast, then looked
again. Still there!

"Don't go away," she whispered.
"Please!"

Luckily Dan was still awake.

"Quick! Come quick!" she hissed.

"Now what?"

"Come *on*!"

She hurried ahead of him.

"Oh no!"

"What?" Dan came up behind her.

"It's gone! But it was there, it was!"

"*What* was?"

She told him. He didn't believe her.
She had not expected him to.

"Seeing things," he told her.

"Seeing double," she said. "Don't you
remember what Mr Tonks said, and
Sam?"

"But they really *did* see double. They saw two, both at the same time. You only saw one. Or think you did."

"I did!"

"What about pink elephants? See any of them?"

She made to kick him, but remembered in time that she had no shoes on.

"Oh *you!*" she said. "Think you know everything. You didn't believe me when I said the egg was getting warm. But it hatched, didn't it?"

"Bit different," Dan said. "Bit different from saying the Gift can be in two places at once."

"I didn't say that! Any case – perhaps he can. He's magic, isn't he?"

"I'm going back to bed. Don't bother waking me next time you start seeing things."

When he had gone Mary stayed by the window for a while, eyes fixed on the dark gleam of the canal. Then, very quietly, she tiptoed along the landing and back down the stairs.

It was what Dan had said, about the Gift being in two places at the same time. If he could do that, perhaps he could magic himself away to wherever he wanted to be. Earlier, he had certainly wanted to go in the canal. He had as good as asked her. She had to be sure.

Gently, very gently, she turned the knob and pushed open the kitchen door.

"Thank goodness!" she breathed. "Oh, thank goodness!"

There he lay, curled on the rug, a shaft of moonlight tipping the ridges of his spine with silver. He was asleep – and dreaming, no doubt, of treacle tart, sausages and pork pies.

It was a relief to find him still there in the morning. Mr Kane let him out, and first of all he tore round and around the garden in mad circles, like a freed prisoner. Next he went straight to the dustbin and nudged off its lid. His head disappeared inside, and there were clatters and bangs as he sorted cabbages leaves and potato peelings from empty tins and bottles.

"He's greener than we are," Dan said. "He's recycling."

"Yuk!" came a voice from above. "Disgusting!"

It was Susie Barber, standing on something so that she could peer over the fence.

"Waste not want not!" came another voice. It was Uncle Fred, come to collect his trailer. "Should know that, young lady."

The Gift's head shot up from the bin. Next minute Uncle Fred's flat cap was on the ground. It was the Gift's way of showing affection.

"Recognizes me, then!" said Uncle Fred, pleased. "Well, you haven't changed, young feller me lad."

He fished in a carrier and fetched out the remains of the kippers he had had for breakfast.

"Ooops! Nearly had my hand off there!"

Out came apples, stale bread and cheese rinds. Uncle Fred certainly knew the way to the Gift's heart.

"Yuk!" said Susie again. "Has it got worms or something?"

"You're the worm round here, Susie Barber!" Mary told her. "Why don't you mind your own business?"

"It woke my mum and dad up last night," said Susie. "My mum says it's a public nuisance."

"My mum says he's a lamb," retorted Mary.

They all went inside. Bacon was frying. The Gift's nose twitched.

"What was all that about, then?" asked Uncle Fred.

They told him.

"Homesick," he said. "Misses his water. Let him in the canal."

"No!" cried Mary. "We daren't. Not yet. What if he goes straight back to Winklesea?"

She did not tell what she had seen last night – or thought she had seen. Now in broad daylight, she was not so sure.

"And outgrown the paddling pool long since," said Mr Kane. "Still, can't have that performance every night. Neighbours *would* complain, and you couldn't blame 'em."

"So what's to do?" Uncle Fred whistled softly through his teeth.

Everyone thought hard.

"Got it!"

They all looked at him.

"He can come fishing, with me! That's the ticket. The lake."

"And us! We'll come as well!" said Mary.

"School – that's where you're going," Mrs Kane told her.

Dan and Mary groaned. They had clean forgotten. The very first day of the Gift's holiday, and they had to go to school!

"It's an idea, Fred, I don't deny," said Mr Kane. "Trouble is, the police don't want him riding round in that trailer."

"Wouldn't have to," said Uncle Fred. "Sunroof."

There was a pause.

"Ah," said Mr Kane. "See what you're getting at."

"Plenty of room. Have the whole car to himself, and his head up through the sunroof."

"Oooh, he'd love that, wouldn't you, my lamb?" Mrs Kane was feeding the Gift with bacon rinds.

Even Mary reluctantly agreed that he probably would. At least lakes did not run down to the sea.

"If you ask me, there'll be even more traffic jams with his head poking up through the roof," Dan said.

"Nothing in the Highway Code about it," said Mr Kane. "And the police never mentioned it. Right you are, then, Fred – the lake it is!"

Five

A Bit of a Mystery

The first day back at school seemed twice as long as usual. There they had to sit, doing sums and working on projects, while all the time the Gift was out there somewhere in the sunshine, helping Uncle Fred to fish.

"P'raps he'll catch more than Uncle Fred does," Mary said to Dan at break. "He's got a much longer neck than a heron."

"Or frighten all the fish into fits," Dan said. "He doesn't exactly act calm."

The water was the Gift's element, his playground. Once in it, he ducked and dived and thrashed his tail till he was haloed in spray – you could hardly see him for it.

At half past three they were first out of school. They ran all the way home. As they turned into Fetter Lane they could see no sign of Uncle Fred's car.

"Not back!"

They were not really surprised. Once Uncle Fred got fishing, he was in a world of his own. Time did not exist. They had begged him to be home by the time school was over.

"Can't promise," he had said. "Fish don't have clocks."

He must still be sitting out there somewhere by the lake, eyes fixed on his line, hypnotised.

"Look!" Dan said. "Mrs Barber! Something's up!"

You could tell that, even at a distance. Mrs Kane and Mrs Bit of This Bit of That were arguing. Dan and Mary ran over.

"You can say that till you're blue in the face!" Mrs Barber was saying. "I saw it with my own eyes, I tell you!"

"Then perhaps you'd better get your eyes tested," said Mrs Kane. "And I will say it again. He's not here!"

"What's up?" Dan asked.

"Ah, there you are. P'raps you'd like to tell Mrs Barber where the Gift is."

"Gone fishing," said Dan promptly.

"With Uncle Fred," added Mary.

"And I tell you he hasn't!" Mrs Barber's voice rose to a shriek. "Lid off the dustbin, rubbish all over everywhere! And walking round the garden bold as brass, sniffing my flowers and squashing my pansies! I *saw* it!"

"Can't have," said Mrs Kane calmly.

"And my lettuce!"

"Can't have."

"Look!" Mary pointed triumphantly up the road.

They all turned.

There was a police car, blue light flashing, and behind it came Uncle Fred's battered old car, with the Gift's long neck rearing up through the sunroof. His head swivelled this way and that, and he looked mightily pleased with himself.

Mrs Barber's jaw dropped. Her eyes popped. Mary almost felt sorry for her.

"There you are — alibi!" said Dan. "And police witnesses!"

"I must be going mad!" Mrs Barber was shaking her head as if to clear it.

"Here we go again!" The police officers were getting out of their car. They were the same two who had escorted the Kanes home yesterday.

"You never said he couldn't ride in a car!" said Mary quickly. "Only the trailer."

"Bet there's nothing about it in the Highway Code!" added Dan.

"I think we'd better get this straight," said One. "No travelling on the public highway at all."

"Unless in an enclosed vehicle," said the other. "A horse box."

"A Gift box!" said Mary.

Uncle Fred was helping the Gift out of his car. To show his gratitude, the Gift promptly knocked off his cap. He evidently remembered the policemen and thought of them as friends, because he bounded along the pavement and knocked their caps off, too.

"It shows he likes you!" said Mary swiftly. For all she knew, you could be arrested for it.

"Allow me to present you with a couple of fish," said Uncle Fred.

"No thank you, sir," said One. "It's not allowed."

"It's bribery!" cried Mrs Bit of This Bit of That. "Why don't you arrest him? And that − that horrible creature!"

"Oh there's no need for that, madam,"

said One. "Harmless enough. Just a bit of a nuisance on the Public Highway."

"Harmless?" shrieked Mrs Barber. "Just you come and look at what it's done to my garden!"

She beckoned the policemen over and they followed her back up the yard.

"Quick!" Dan and Mary raced to the back and stood on the garden bench to peer over the fence.

"There!"

The dustbin had certainly been knocked over. There were empty bottles and tins everywhere.

"And there!" She pointed to a few scrappy tufts to show where there had been a row of lettuce.

"So you think the — er — creature did this?"

"Think? I know it did! Saw it with my own eyes!"

"And when exactly did this — er — crime take place?"

"This afternoon! Three o'clock it was — I

know that exact, because that's when I
sit down for a cup of tea and a read of
my paper. And I'd just got the teapot
warmed, and was—"

"Three o'clock?" interrupted One.
"Wasn't it just about then when we

picked 'em up, just outside Haslam?"

"It certainly was," replied Two. "So I'm afraid you're mistaken, madam."

"Cast iron alibi," agreed One.

"So who did that?" she screeched, pointing at her vandalised lettuce.

"Er – greenfly?" suggested Two.

"Oh, and I suppose greenfly knock dustbins over?"

"I don't know about that, madam. Not much of a gardener."

"And I suppose I can't believe my own eyes?"

Neither policeman said anything.

"Mind you, if I was seeing things it'd be no wonder! Hardly a wink of sleep did I get last night! Worse than a tomcat, howling and screeching!"

"It's not true!"

All three turned to see Dan and Mary's heads above the fence.

"He only howled for a minute or two!"

"Because he was homesick!"

"And we brought him straight inside and he never made another sound."

"Woke us up, anyhow," said Mrs Barber. "You can't deny that. It's a public nuisance."

"Did anyone else complain?" asked One, looking at Dan and Mary.

"No!" they replied in chorus.

"Are you going to charge it or not?" demanded Mrs Barber.

"It woke *me* up as well!" It was Susie, home from school. Dan and Mary could have killed her.

"If it was just the one occasion, there's nothing much we can do about it," the police officers said, making a hasty exit.

You could tell whose side the police were on. They turned and went. Mary stuck out her tongue at Susie and jumped off the seat. Dan followed.

When Mr Kane got back from work they told him all about it.

"Bit of a mystery, that," he said. "Swears she *saw* him, you say?"

"Yes, except that she keeps calling him 'it' and she's just trying to get him into trouble," Dan said. "I expect it was rabbits that ate her lettuce."

"Though it'd be a powerful big rabbit could knock a dustbin over," said Mr Kane thoughtfully.

Still Mary said not a word about what she had seen last night – or thought she had seen. For one thing, she had a plan.

"What about the Gift tonight?" she asked. "Will he sleep out or in?"

"Seems settled enough now, bless his heart," said Mrs Kane. "Had a nice splash round with Fred, didn't you my lamb?"

"The police said it wasn't a public nuisance if he just howled once," Dan said. "But what if he does it again?"

"Ought really be out in the fresh air," said Mr Kane. "Not natural, cooped up inside."

"I've had an idea," said Mary. "Dan and me could sleep in the tent and keep him company."

"Oooh, it's getting a bit backendish for that," said Mrs Kane dubiously. "Catch your deaths . . ."

"You always say that," Dan told her. "We haven't caught our deaths yet."

"I reckon that's a good idea, our Mary," said Mr Kane. "Just the ticket. Bit of company for him, just while he settles in."

"You don't want those horrible Barbers complaining to the Council," said Mary cunningly.

"Oh, go on, then," said Mrs Kane. "Just this once."

So the tent was fetched out from the cupboard under the stairs, and the poles and pegs from the shed.

Putting it up took longer than it should have done, because the Gift evidently thought it was some new kind of game. The first time they put up the pole, the Gift promptly knocked it down again, and ended up with his head smothered under the canvas. He struggled to free

himself and all the pegs came out as he lurched about the garden with the tent still over his head.

"Lots of sleep we're going to get if he keeps doing that," Dan said.

"No!" said Mary firmly. "No! Bad boy!"

The Gift knew what that meant, all right. He hung his head and looked so crestfallen that Mary gave him the rhubarb bucket to play with while she and Dan sorted out the tent.

The best part of camping out in the garden was round about half past ten, when Mr and Mrs Kane went to bed. Not once had Dan and Mary ever fallen asleep before then. They had a torch each, and books and playing cards, or lay back in the darkness talking and telling jokes.

Then came the magical moment when they would see the lights go off in the house, one by one, and the real camping began. Then, after a short wait, just to make sure that lights did not go on again, came the midnight feast.

This occasion, of course, was rather different. For one thing, the Gift could not make out what was going on. He didn't uproot the tent again, but he did keep nudging it, and peering in through the flap.

"He can probably smell the food," Dan said. "Roll on half past ten!"

Mary said nothing. She was thinking not of the feast, but of that shadowy shape out there on the canal. Soon, perhaps, the mystery would be solved.

Six

A Visitor

At last the lights of Number Seventeen Fetter Lane went off one by one. Dan and Mary crouched in their tent and watched. Only one was left, upstairs. Now and then they saw shadows move across the curtains. Mr and Mrs Kane were getting ready for bed.

Then at last that light went out, too, and in the same instant the moon appeared from behind a cloud.

"Hurray!" breathed Mary, remembering another strange, moonlit picnic in the sand dunes.

"Wait five minutes!" Dan whispered. "Make sure they're asleep!"

Mr and Mrs Kane were very sound sleepers, and neither had any trouble dropping off.

Dan and Mary played a whispered game of *I Spy* to pass those last long minutes. Then Dan said "I spy with my little eye something beginning with . . . M!" and Mary promptly guessed "Midnight Feast — except that it isn't!"

That hardly mattered, as they pulled the rug out from the tent and spread it on the grass. The Gift watched, head tilted to one side.

They had crawled back into the tent to fetch the food when they heard the first whimper.

"Oh no!" Mary seized an apple and scrambled back out. The Gift was still sitting, head tilted, but curiously stiffened, as if listening.

Again there came that soft whimper.

"Stop him, can't you!" came Dan's muffled voice.

But Mary too was frozen, staring at the Gift. Whoever had made that sound, it was not he.

Then came another sound. A rattling. Mary looked towards the gate that led to the canal bank, and actually saw the latch move.

So, evidently, did the Gift. With a few bounds he was there, nudging the latch, butting the fence with his head.

Slowly, very slowly, Mary followed.

"Whatever?" She heard Dan's voice behind her.

"Sssh! There's someone out there!"

She was close enough now to the gate to see the key, left as usual in the lock. She knew what she must do. Her heart thudded.

There was nothing really to be frightened of. She already thought she knew who — or what — was out there. But if so, then it would be like seeing lightening strike in the same place twice, or a blue moon.

She took a deep breath. Then, reaching past the Gift's ridged back, felt the cold of the key at her fingertips. She turned it. The gate swung slowly open.

Mary gasped. For an instant she glimpsed a mirror image of the Gift, and then the Gift himself was past her, and greeting this uninvited visitor.

That the pair knew one another was not in doubt. They eagerly craned their long necks and nuzzled, their tails swished and beat from side to side. Their moon silvered eyes gazed into one another's, barely inches apart. From deep in their throats came soft little moans of pure delight. It seemed as if they would stay like that forever, entranced. It was as if they would never come apart.

And all that long while Dan and Mary gazed at this strangest love scene since the Owl and the Pussycat's courtship on the sands. It would hardly have surprised them if along the whitened towpath a piggywig had strolled, with a ring at the end of his nose, his nose, with a ring at the end of his nose.

They stared long enough to notice that the Gift's lady love was not grey, but what looked like a pale, greenish gold. It was hard to tell. Moonlight bleached and altered colours, even their own faces were turned to wax. She was smaller than the Gift, too, but the real difference was in her head. Where the Gift's was smooth, hers had a circle of small ridges, as if she were wearing a coronet.

She was beautiful, Mary could see that. And she felt a pang of jealousy, because she knew that part of the Gift was now lost to her forever. He had been their playmate, an outsized pet from another world. Never again would he be content simply with bowling dustbin lids, rides in the wheelbarrow, plates of chips. He had gone to a place where they could not follow.

It would have been no surprise to her if the pair had finally slipped into the sleek water of the canal and headed for the sea. Surely that was why this visitor had come – to bring the Gift back to Winklesea?

But when, at last, the pair drew apart, it was not towards the canal they turned, but Dan and Mary. There was the happy, familiar face of the Gift, and there was this other face, which they now saw plain for the first time. Big dark eyes, curling whiskers, a wide mouth that was surely smiling, all topped by that neat little coronet.

She craned forward, and gave them both a soft nudge, first Mary, then Dan.

"O wow!" Dan said. "She likes us!"

The Gift himself pushed them both aside and went back into the garden. The visitor followed.

"I don't believe it!" Dan whispered.

"I told you! I told you!"

"She's got a kind of crown. Is she a queen, or something?"

"That's it — Queenie! Let's call her that!"

Back in the garden, the Gift seemed to be showing off his own kingdom.

"Is she going to *stay*?"

"Don't know. Look — he hasn't forgotten the feast!"

The apple that Mary had dropped still lay there, a moon apple. The Gift bowled it over the grass so that it rolled right to the feet - or rather, flippers - of his guest. She bent her neck. Snap! It had gone. Queen or not, she was evidently in the same league as the Gift himself when it came to eating.

By now the Gift's own head had disappeared inside the tent.

"Quick — or he'll scoff the lot!"

And so there were four at the feast instead of three. There was enough to

eat only because the Gift was sharing with
Queenie. He even shared his biscuits.

Dan and Mary were still in a daze,
their minds racing. Had Queenie come
to stay? If so, how on earth would they
feed her? And what would the neighbours say? Had Queenie hatched out on
somebody else's mantelpiece?

They asked none of these questions
out loud. The Gift could not speak,
but they were absolutely certain that he
understood every single word they said.
It seemed likely that so would Queenie,
too.

In any case, they felt curiously shy with
this uninvited guest. It was as if she were
a grown up at a children's party, and
they had to mind their manners.

Once the food had all gone they sat
silent, at a loss. What now? They had
meant to have games with the Gift –
Pig in the Middle, and rides in the
wheelbarrow. What they were dreading
was that the Gift and Queenie would go

back through the still open gate, into the canal and away down to Winklesea, gone forever.

It was the Gift who decided matters. He turned and went toward the potting shed. The door was ajar.

"If it rains, you go in there," Mr Kane had told them. "Don't you come banging on the door in the middle of the night, thank you very much."

The Gift nudged the door wide open. Queenie went and peered past him. She hesitated for a moment, then went in.

"O wow!" whispered Dan. "She's stopping!"

The Gift himself flopped down by the door and rested his chin on the step. He shut his eyes.

"Come on!" whispered Mary.

They left the remains of their feast still scattered on the rug and crawled back into the tent. Now at last the questions could be asked, even if only in whispers.

"Why's she come?"

"How did she know where we were?"

"So that's why he wanted to stay in Winklesea!"

"And why he made that racket last night."

"Oh Dan, she's his own true love!"

"Oh yuk! Girls!"

"She is, she is! Oh Dan, the Gift must have gone and grown up without us noticing!"

"Grown up? You're joking!"

But the Gift had grown up, or at

any rate had stopped growing. He had
done that long ago. At the time of his
disappearance Uncle Fred had predicted
he would end up the size of a house.
But when they had met him again in
Winklesea he was still the same size as
when they had last seen him.

"He likes her better than he likes us!"
At last she had said it. She had known it
from the first moment, could hardly bear
it.

"Let him, then! Who cares?" Dan
pulled up his sleeping bag and turned
away his head.

So he knew, too. Mary lay for a long
while, blinking away the tears.

Queenie had come up the long canal
from Winklesea to Fetter Lane, and the
world would never be the same again. It
was the end of a chapter.

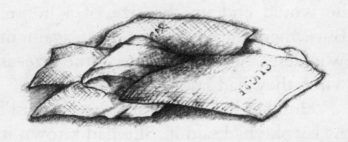

Seven

Gone!

Almost in the instant of waking, Mary remembered. She smelled the cold dew, saw canvas instead of ceiling, and was still blinking as she crawled through the flap of the tent.

Her eyes went straight to the shed. The Gift was not there. She staggered over, her legs still heavy with sleep, and peered in.

Gone! There was the crumpled pile of sacks where Queenie had lain.

Slowly Mary turned and with a huge sickness knew what she would see. Last night they had not even bothered to clear the remains of the feast. They had also left the gate open.

"Oh no! Oh Winkie!"

That the Gift should have gone was bad enough, but to have lost him again through their own carelessness was unbearable. Fiercely and hopelessly she willed the clock to turn back, to play that moonlit scene again, exactly the same but with that one difference, that one extra act of shutting and locking the gate.

"Oh, if only . . ."

She ran to the gate, still hoping. The canal curved away on the seaward side so she could not see very far. It lay blank and shining with not so much as a ripple, holding only the sky.

Brushing her sleeve across her eyes

she went back into the garden. As she
did so she heard the back door being
unlocked, and her father's voice.

"Morning, campers! Wakey wakey,
rise and shine!"

Dan's head poked through the flap.

"Dan! They've gone!"

"What?"

"We left the gate open. They've
gone!"

"Oh yes, what's this – midnight feast?
Where's he, then? Gone for a swim?
Working up an appetite for breakfast?"

"Oh Dad!" Mary burst into tears.

All at once Mrs Kane was there too,
still in her dressing gown, and the whole
story came tumbling out.

Along with the shock of the Gift's
disappearance, Mr and Mrs Kane had to
take in the news that he was not the only
creature of his kind in the world. At first,
they were inclined to think that Dan and
Mary must have been dreaming.

"What – both having the same dream?"

Dan said. "You can't. Dreams are private."

"And remember what Mr Tonks and Sam said about seeing double," Mary said. "They must have seen her without knowing. And it must've been her Mrs Barber saw yesterday."

"Her?" said Mr Kane. "Why *her*?"

Mary explained as best she could. Impossible now, in broad daylight, to conjure up that pale creature with her jaunty coronet.

"And anyway, they were kissing!" she finished.

"Pass the sick bag!" Dan said.

"They were! You know they were!"

At this Mrs Kane felt the strong need for a sit down and a nice cup of tea. Her pet lamb, her baby, had grown up overnight and left the nest. She could not take it in.

"Fetch the milk, Mary," she said. "And to think − I ordered an extra pint for him."

The three bottles stood by the front
step. So did something else. There were
two plastic carriers and a bucket, full
of scraps. The neighbours were already
making their offerings to the Gift, just as
they had the last time. It was partly to save

having their dustbins knocked over.

"Pity you never shut that gate," Mr Kane was saying when she got back to the kitchen.

"And after all that trouble you went to to make it." Mrs Kane was pouring the tea with expert swoops.

"*I* don't think so," Mary said.

They all looked at her.

"He was never meant to be a prisoner," she said. "He stopped here because he liked it."

Now, it seemed, he no longer did.

"And think how lonely he must have felt — everybody having two legs except him! *And* he didn't have anyone to talk to. He was talking to her, you could tell he was."

"Knew what we were saying, though," observed Mr Kane. "Every word."

"It's not the same! Just *you* try not being able to talk!"

She herself had once decided to go all day without opening her eyes, to find out how it felt to be blind. The experiment had lasted hardly an hour.

"Not manners, though, going off like that," said Mrs Kane. "I'm surprised at him."

"P'raps he'll send a postcard when he gets to Winklesea," Dan said. "Ha ha!"

He was just as upset as Mary, she knew that. The welcome home banner had been his idea.

"I should've liked to've met his lady friend," Mrs Kane continued. "Pretty, you say she was, Mary?"

"Beautiful," said Mary. She had to admit it. "We were going to call her Queenie."

The back door opened and in came Uncle Fred.

"Bit early in the day for callers, Fred," said Mr Kane.

"Going fishing. Just called in to see how the little chap is. Settled in, has he?"

No one replied. Mary, for one, could

not bear to go through the whole story again.

"Where is he?"

Mary went back out into the garden. Susie Barber was peering over the fence.

"Where is it?" she asked.

"He, not it, if you don't mind," Mary told her. "Never you mind."

"Run off, I bet," Susie said. "Don't blame it. Good riddance."

"Just because *your* mother won't let you have a pet."

"I'm saving up for a pony, so there!" said Susie.

In a way, you couldn't help feeling sorry for her.

"My mum was going to report it to the council, anyway," she went on.

"If you say that once more, I'll – I'll–" Mary did not know what she would do. In any case, it didn't matter now.

She had meant simply to stick out her tongue and walk away. Then she noticed Susie's face. Her eyes were fixed on something beyond, and stretched wider and wider. Her mouth started to open and close like that of a fish. It was very interesting. All at once the face abruptly disappeared, and there was a clatter as whatever she had been standing on fell over.

Mary turned. She felt her own eyes stretch wider and wider. *Her* mouth opened and closed.

"Mum!" she screamed at last. "Dad!"

The Gift was there again, and behind him came Queenie. By daylight you could see that she really was a pale greenish gold. She looked delicious, like something you could lick.

The pair looked uncommonly pleased with themselves. They seemed to be smiling.

"Well I never!" said Mrs Kane faintly.

"Wow!" said Dan.

"I'll go to the foot of our stairs!" said Uncle Fred.

"Now who's seeing double?" said Mr Kane.

They all were. There, in their ordinary little back garden, were two creatures of magic, stretching their long necks and looking hopefully at the polestruck Kanes. A pair of startled blackbirds watched from the fence.

"Isn't she pretty!" said Mrs Kane. "What a lamb!"

Now she had two lambs.

"You never know what you'll find next when you come to this house," observed Uncle Fred. "Put in your thumb and out comes a plum!"

The Gift seemed to like that, because he came over and knocked Uncle Fred's cap off. He beamed at the others. If they had had caps, he would have knocked those off, too.

Queenie did not move. She hung back, as if uncertain of her welcome. The Kanes themselves felt awkward. After all, they had known the Gift since he was a baby.

She had come into their lives as a stranger, fully fledged. And that little coronet on her sleek head really did make them feel as if they were in the presence of royalty.

"Would they like something to eat, do you think?" said Mrs Kane.

"Ask a silly question," said Uncle Fred.

"Wait!" Mary sped round to the front door and picked up the pail of scraps.

"There!" she plonked it in front of the pair.

"All contributions gratefully received," said Uncle Fred.

The Gift's nose did not dive straight into the pail as they had expected. Instead, he inclined his head towards Queenie, inviting her to go first.

"Proper little gentleman!" exclaimed Mrs Kane admiringly.

"Must be seeing things," said Uncle Fred. "Eat a house, that one would, if it was made of bacon rinds."

"Or chips," said Mr Kane.

"Or biscuits," added Dan.

Still Queenie did not move. They all stood there, waiting. Mary found herself holding her breath. It seemed somehow hugely important that Queenie should eat her offering. It would be a sign – a sign that she wanted to stay.

"What's the matter with her?" Dan whispered.

"Mostly peelings by the look of it," said Mr Kane. "Don't fancy peelings much myself."

It was not that. The Gift never turned up his nose at anything. Dustbin Dan Mr Kane sometimes called him.

"I know what I think," said Mrs Kane. "I think the poor little thing's frightened, and no wonder. Bless her heart – come all that long way up the canal from Winklesea."

"And five of us stood here gawping at her," said Uncle Fred.

"Come on, my little duck!" Now Mrs Kane had a duck as well as a lamb. She went right up to Queenie, who cowered away and hunched up against the Gift, as if for comfort. "Don't you be frightened, it's only me. Here – have a nice bit of cabbage, will you?"

She delved into the pail and held out a cabbage stalk. With the other hand she gently stroked the timid creature's neck.

"Ooh, aren't you soft? Softer than that little rascal! Come on then – nice cabbage. Come on, ducky!"

They waited. Then – snap! All at once the cabbage stalk had gone.

"Ought to take up lion taming," said Uncle Fred.

Once Queenie had started, there was no stopping her. She and the Gift dipped into the pail, turn and turn about. Crusts, stale cake, peelings, all went into those steadily working jaws in swift succession till the pail was empty.

"Right. That was breakfast," said Uncle Fred. "Now – what's for dinner?"

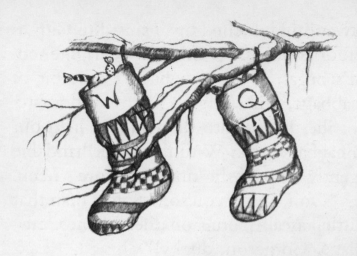

*E*ight

Gifts Galore

"I've got tummy ache," said Mary.

"And I think I've got a sore throat coming," Dan said.

"And I think my head's working loose," said Mr Kane. "School, both of you!"

"I think it's educational," Dan said. "No one else in the whole world has ever had a Gift, let alone two. It's historical."

It was hopeless, of course. Off to

school they had to go. To make matters worse, Mrs Bit of This Bit of That was at the gate again as they went.

"You might as well live next door to a zoo,' she said. "Two of the horrible things now. Nine o'clock sharp I ring the council. It's against the bye laws. Must be."

"I hate her," Mary said. "She's a toilet."

"And I hate school," Dan said. "It's a double toilet."

All day long those two magical creatures would be frolicking in their garden, and they would not be there to see it. It was like being told that they would miss Christmas.

"I wish I'd never said that about leaving the gate open," Mary said. "You don't think they will, do you?"

She did not want to be a jailer, keep Winkie and Queenie against their will. Nor did she want to get home from school and find them gone.

When at last they did go racing round

the corner and into Fetter Lane, the first
thing they saw was a police car. It was
parked outside Number Seventeen.

"Oh no! That horrible Barber!"

But what they found was not the Gift
and Queenie being arrested. The same
two policemen who had escorted the
Gift home were out in the garden, taking
photos. They both had cameras, and were
taking photos of the Gift and Queenie,
and Mrs Kane was taking photos of them
taking photos.

"Wow! I'll get my camera!" Dan
wanted to take photos of Mrs Kane taking
photos of the police taking photos.

The Gift and Queenie posed obligingly.
They peered from behind hollyhocks,
they gazed into one another's eyes, and
all the cameras went click click click. It
was like a wedding.

"Arrest them!" It was Mrs Barber over
the fence, and she had her camera too.
She was collecting evidence. She was
taking photos of Dan taking photos of

Mrs Kane taking photos of the police taking photos of the Gift and Queenie.

"Sorry, madam," said One. "Off duty."

"Not doing a lot of harm," said Two. "Not vandalising phone boxes or wrecking bus shelters or joyriding."

The police were as enchanted with the new arrival as the Kanes themselves. It turned out that they wanted the Gift to be their station mascot. They thought he would bring them luck, cut the crime rate by half probably. Now it seemed they would have two mascots.

"Double mascot, double luck," said Two. "*Where* did you say you'd found him?"

So they were taken into the house to see the bluish green — or greenish blue — stone egg on the mantelpiece between the clock and the green glass cat. They took photos of that, too.

Then the Gift was there with Queenie, and the little living room was suddenly crowded. He led her over to the mantelpiece. He looked first at the egg, then at her. She craned her long neck and peered at it. Her head tilted this way and that. She nudged it gently, and it rocked on its cockleshell base. And all the time the pair were making little purring noises, deep in their throats.

The police did not purr. They were gobsmacked. They simply could not get over it.

"He came out of *there*?"

"Ever so tiny he was," nodded Mrs Kane. "Not much bigger than a mouse."

"Big enough to wolf a chip down the minute he was born," Dan said. "We should've called him Jaws. Would've, if we'd known."

"It's going to be a bit of a worry, feeding the two of them," said Mrs Kane. "They've already had all those scraps from the neighbours."

"No problem," said One.

"We'll have a whip round at the station," said Two.

So that is what happened. The Gift and Queenie were made official mascots of Newark police. A fund was set up for buying broken biscuits and out of date stock from supermarkets. And every day a police car would draw up in front of Number Seventeen Fetter Lane with bags of scraps from the lads at the station.

The police arranged a signal, to let their mascots know they were coming. A pip on the horn and two quick bursts on the siren. By the time the police got out of their car with the day's offerings, the Gift and Queenie were there, peering eagerly over the yard gate.

They were getting food from somewhere else, too. It was Mary who spotted it. She looked out of her bedroom window one morning, as she always did, first thing. She could never quite take magic for granted. Each day she would breathe a huge sigh of relief to see the pair still there.

This particular day they were side by

side, gazing up at the garden fence. As she watched, something flew through the air and Queenie stretched her neck and caught it – snap!

"One for you, now one for *you*!"

A chunk of cake was there one minute, gone the next. Over the top of the fence Mary saw the face of Susie Barber.

"Good boy, Winkie! Now – Queenie!"

Another slab of cake. Susie Barber, whose mother wouldn't let her have a pet, had adopted one – or rather, two.

Once it was decided that Queenie had
settled in, the Kanes left the garden gate
ajar during the daytime. At first Mary had
been nervous about this.

"What if they go round dustbins being a public nuisance?" she said.

"Dustbins?" said Mr Kane. "With all
the food they're getting? If the police
carry on like this they'll bust, the pair
of them."

So the Gift and Queenie could dive
into the canal whenever they wished.
They spent hours there, ducking and div-
ing, making waves.

As Christmas drew near, the weather
turned cold and frosty.

"Time to come inside," Mrs Kane
decided. "Can't have the lambs with
chilblains."

"No toes," said Uncle Fred. He was
spending a lot of time at Fetter Lane
these days. You can't fish in frozen lakes.
"No toes – no chilblains. Still – could get
frozen flippers."

So every night the Gift and Queenie came into the warm kitchen, and every day the gate to the canal was kept shut. At first there was only a thin film of ice over the water, but as the days passed it grew thicker.

"Can't have 'em jumping on it and it cracking," Mr Kane said. "Dangerous, that."

"I shouldn't think they know about ice," Mary said. "The sea never freezes over. Imagine that – frozen waves!"

Each day Mr Kane went out and tested the ice.

"Not yet," he would say. "Give it another day or two."

What the whole family were hoping was that one day the ice *would* be thick enough, and the Gift and Queenie could be let out there.

"They'll think it's magic," Mary said. "What'll they do, I wonder? Slip? Slide? Skate?"

"Or go flat on their bums!" Dan said.

It was Christmas Day itself when they found out. In the morning there were stockings for the Gift and Queenie, as well as the children. Uncle Fred had had his doubts about this.

"No legs, no stockings," he had said.

"If the police say stockings, stockings it is," Mr Kane had told him. "The law, you might say."

The police at Newark station had done the pair proud. First, they had invited them to their own children's Christmas party. They sent a Black Maria to fetch them, and Dan and Mary went, too. So did Susie Barber, who was quite human these days. There was not so much as a squeak from Mrs Bit of This Bit of That.

The Gift and Queenie were stars of the party, they even eclipsed Santa Claus himself. Most of the children went home and added an extra item to their letters to Santa Claus, right at the top of the list.

Afterwards the police delivered their

guests safely home, all wearing paper hats and with bags of sweets.

"Should the Gift and Queenie have stockings?" Mary had asked them.

"Definitely," they said. "In fact, it's the law. And they might get another surprise, I shouldn't wonder."

So on Christmas morning the Gift and Queenie first watched Dan and Mary empty their stockings. Then they were led outside into the frosty garden, where their own stockings hung from the whitened boughs of the cherry tree. First they had to knock them off, with excited buttings of the head and nudges with the nose. The hoar frost showered about them.

Then the stockings were down, and out came the chocolate, biscuits, apples. Mary had wanted to put a tangerine in the toe, and a shiny new coin. Mr Kane had vetoed this.

"Swallow 'em whole, I shouldn't wonder," he had said. "And Christmas

Day at the vet's, having 'em X rayed."

At the rate the pair were scoffing, he was probably right. The Gift nearly swallowed a squeaky frog by mistake, and an india rubber ball.

"One thing, they won't manage much turkey," said Mr Kane.

"Merry Christmas, all!"

There were the two policemen, whose names had turned out to be Steve and Colin. Their caps were trimmed with tinsel and holly.

"Surprise!"

They stepped forward, and behind them was the biggest sledge anyone had ever seen. It was big enough for a pony – or a Gift from Winklesea.

"From all the lads at the station!" said Steve.

"Helped make it myself," said Colin. "Like it?"

The Gift went over. First he knocked off their caps, then he sniffed at the sledge.

"Probably hopes it's made of chocolate," Dan said.

"I'll show you!"

Mary went and sat on the sledge. The police pulled it. Woosh it went over the frozen grass, and the Gift, with a whoop of excitement, climbed on behind her. Whoop whoop whoop he went as the sledge moved forward.

Mr Kane called from the canal bank, where he had gone to do his daily testing.

"Hard as a rock!" he shouted. "Hold an elephant!"

And so there were winter sports at Fetter Lane that day. Even Uncle Fred joined in.

The garden gate had been kept shut for days. When the Gift and Queenie first tried to dive into the canal they skidded half way across it on their noses.

But once they had got the hang of it they turned out to be born skaters. They swooped and skimmed and glided and their high whoops rang out in the frosty air. They towed the sledge so fast that Dan and Mary felt they were flying, and Uncle Fred fell off more than once.

They all went in for Christmas dinner, and afterwards were straight out there again, with the Gift and Queenie leading the way.

"It won't last forever," Mary told them. "Things never do. Especially ice."

They stayed out till the frost began to fall again and the sun was a glowing orange disc beyond the gasworks.

"That was the best day of my life," Mary said, as they trooped back through the darkening garden. "There'll never be another day like this in my whole life."

She should have known better. When the Gift from Winklesea was around, anything could happen. And later, when spring came to Fetter Lane and the days began to lengthen, it did.

At first they all thought Queenie was not well. One day she would not come out of the shed when the first bucket of scraps was brought into the garden. They tried to coax her.

"Come along, my ducky!" Mrs Kane dangled crispy bacon rinds, her favourite.

Queenie did not budge. She simply sat there on her heap of sacks, her eyes bright and fastened on the rinds. When they were placed in front of her she snapped them up in a trice.

"Can't be that poorly," said Mrs Kane, and went to fry more bacon.

Queenie stayed in the shed all day. They brought her food, and the Gift himself picked out the choicest morsels and laid them before her.

When she stayed there the next day, and the next, Mr Kane began to wonder if they should call in the vet.

"Though I don't know what he'd make of it," he said. "Not exactly your tabby cat, is she, or your poodle?"

The other odd thing was that Queenie seemed to be purring – or gurgling – or crooning. For hours on end she sat there in the dusty dimness, plump and contented, cooing like a dove.

Then, one early April morning, the Kanes were awakened by the sound of the Gift's whooping. Blackbirds were whistling, the sun streaming through the curtains and the Gift – whooping.

"Whatever?"

They scrambled out of bed and down the stairs and out into the sunlit garden. The Gift was performing a kind of dance, he was making patterns in the dew and arching his neck and uttering strange, high sounds such as they had never heard before.

As soon as he saw them he lollopped towards them and gave them eager nudges that nearly knocked them over (and would certainly have knocked off their caps, had they been wearing them).

He turned then, and strutted towards the shed and the dew flashed from his flippers. As he did so, Queenie stepped out into the sunlight, all delicious greeny gold and singing, positively singing.

"She's better!" gasped Mary.

"I reckon they want to show us something," said Mr Kane.

The pair were standing by the open door of the shed and leaning against one another, and gazing.

Slowly the Kanes went forward, and

peered in. At first, eyes still dazzled by the sun, they saw nothing but the familiar clutter of lawnmower, tools, plantpots. On the floor was the pile of sacks where Queenie had made her nest. And on those sacks . . .

"I don't believe it!" Mary felt a shiver run straight down her spine, and up, and down again.

"Oh wow!" Dan whispered. "Wow!"

There on the crumpled sacks lay an egg. It was bluish green – or greenish blue – and the only egg like it they had ever seen was the one that had stood on a cockleshell pedestal with A Gift From Winklesea painted in beautiful gold letters.

Magic had come to stay at Number Seventeen Fetter Lane.

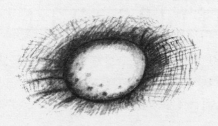

ORDER FORM

0 340 64642 X   A GIFT FROM WINKLESEA £2.99 ☐
                Helen Cresswell

0 340 64648 9   WHATEVER HAPPENED   £8.99 ☐
                IN WINKLESEA?
                Helen Cresswell (hardback)

All Hodder Children's books are available at your local bookshop or newsagent, or can be ordered direct from the publisher. Just tick the titles you want and fill in the form below. Prices and availability subject to change without notice.

Hodder Children's Books, Cash Sales Department, Bookpoint, 39 Milton Park, Abingdon, OXON, OX14 4TD, UK. If you have a credit card you may order by telephone – (01235) 831700.

Please enclose a cheque or postal order made payable to Bookpoint Ltd to the value of the cover price and allow the following for postage and packing: UK & BFPO – £1.00 for the first book, 50p for the second book and 30p for each additional book ordered up to a maximum charge of £3.00.
OVERSEAS & EIRE – £2.00 for the first book, £1.00 for the second book and 50p for each additional book.

Name ....

Address ....

....

....

If you would prefer to pay by credit card, please complete:
Please debit my Visa/Access/Diner's Card/American Express (delete as applicable) card no:

Signature ....

Expiry Date ....